SARAH J HEIDELBERG

INK-SMUDGED LOVE

First published by Ophelia Brown Publishing via IngramSpark 2024

First edition

This book was professionally typeset on Reedsy.
Find out more at reedsy.com

Contents

1

The Lost Pages

Eliza Monroe crouched on the sodden ground, her fingers trembling as she gently lifted the damp, mud-streaked pages of her cherished diary. Hurricane Katrina had ravaged her world, scattering her belongings across the decimated landscape of her Mississippi hometown. The vibrant, handwritten words of her youth were now smeared and blurred, yet she clung to them with an unyielding resolve to salvage fragments of her past.

The acrid scent of dampness and decay permeated the air as Eliza sat by the space heater in the dimly lit living room. She meticulously laid out the fragile pages, watching as the heat coaxed the remaining moisture from the paper. Her father's heavy footsteps echoed through the hollow shell of their once lively home, and soon, he appeared in the doorway, his face a tapestry of worry and fatigue.

"Eliza, what on earth are you doing?" he asked, his voice thick with concern.

She looked up, her eyes reflecting a blend of determination and sorrow. "I'm trying to save these, Dad. They hold so many memories."

Her father sighed deeply, the weight of their shared grief pressing down on him. He lowered himself onto the worn-out couch beside her. "I understand, sweetheart, but you can't hold onto everything. Some things… some things have to be let go."

Eliza's grip on the delicate pages tightened. "Not these. They're too important."

Her father watched her for a moment, his eyes softening with empathy. He knew better than to argue. Eliza's bond with her diaries was profound, each page a testament to her inner world and her journey through life.

As the pages dried, she carefully slid them into protective plastic sleeves, feeling a sense of triumph despite the overwhelming loss surrounding her. Later that evening, she sat on her bed, the salvaged pages spread before her. With a tender touch, she began to read, each word transporting her back to her childhood.

She was ten years old again, seated at the family computer, typing furiously to her mysterious online friend. Their conversations had been her sanctuary, a place where she could express her dreams, fears, and burgeoning sense of self. She had saved every word, each dialogue a precious link to a simpler time.

In the flickering glow of the bedside lamp, Eliza lost herself in the past. She remembered the thrill of their first conversation, the way her heart had raced with excitement. Her friend had been a guiding light, offering wisdom and understanding beyond his years. Little did she know that he was a pop star, hidden behind the anonymity of the internet, sharing his thoughts with a young girl who idolized him without ever realizing his true identity.

Outside, the night was still and quiet, a stark contrast to the chaos that had torn through their lives. The silence was heavy, filled with unspoken fears and unvoiced hopes. Eliza's father stood in the hallway, watching her through the cracked door. He saw the way her face softened as she read, the way her eyes sparkled with nostalgia. He knew that these pages were more than just paper; they were pieces of her heart, fragments of a life that had been irrevocably changed.

As Eliza read, she felt a sense of peace settle over her. The memories were bittersweet, but they were hers. They were proof that she had lived, that she had loved and been loved. In those pages, she found the strength to face the uncertain future, to rebuild her life from the ruins.

Her father's voice broke the silence, gentle and tentative. "Eliza, are you coming to bed?"

She looked up, smiling softly. "In a little while, Dad. I just need a few more minutes."

He nodded, understanding. "Take your time, sweetheart."

Eliza returned to her reading, her heart full of gratitude for the moments she had managed to save. She knew that the road ahead would be difficult, that there would be more losses to endure. But for now, she had these pages, these memories. And that was enough.

In the quiet of the night, Eliza Monroe made a silent vow to herself. She would not let the storm define her. She would hold onto the past, but she would also embrace the future, carrying the lessons and the love of those who had come before her. And in doing so, she would find her way forward, one step at a time.

2

Life in Kansas

Eliza Monroe's life took another unexpected turn when she found her father unresponsive one morning, his face pallid and his breathing shallow. The ambulance's wail was still ringing in her ears when she got the call from her brother James. His voice was tight with concern. "Eliza, we need to get Dad the care he needs. You have to move here immediately."

The decision was agonizing. Eliza cherished her home in Mississippi, despite the devastation Hurricane Katrina had wreaked upon it. But with the climate shifting and the COVID-19 pandemic threatening, staying was no longer viable.

Packing was a frantic and sorrowful ordeal. Eliza's heart ached as she sifted through her belongings, longing to take everything, especially her diaries and the precious pages she had painstakingly saved from the hurricane's wrath. Yet, with limited space and time, James urged her to prioritize essentials. It felt like tearing pieces of her heart apart.

The journey to Kansas was long and filled with reflection. Eliza's car was packed to the brim, the road stretching out before her like a gray ribbon. Her father's labored breathing filled the silence, a constant reminder of their urgency. The Mississippi landscape gave way to the barren expanses of the southwest, their journey taking them past curious landmarks and small towns.

As they neared the desert, Eliza's thoughts turned to her enigmatic friend Nate. She vividly recalled a concert where, despite being seated in the balcony, she had felt as though she was floating onto the stage when he called for volunteers. That ethereal night had solidified her connection to him, even though his true identity remained a mystery.

When they passed a sign for Area 51, Eliza couldn't help but feel a shiver of intrigue. The mysterious aura of the place seemed to resonate with her own life's uncertainties. She glanced at her father, who was dozing fitfully, and wondered if the answers to her own mysteries lay somewhere out there, hidden and elusive.

Kansas greeted Eliza with a mix of relief and melancholy. The new home was a sprawling brick and mortar house, its whitewashed walls and wide porches a stark contrast to the intimate, weathered charm of her Mississippi abode. Not all her belongings had made it, deepening her sense of loss. She missed her blue house, which had been repainted and restored without her knowledge. It stood as a symbol of her slipping past, a tether to memories now drifting further away.

Her father's condition demanded most of her attention in the initial days. The hospital visits, the medical jargon, the somber faces of the healthcare professionals—all of it was overwhelming. Eliza felt as though she was swimming against a powerful current, trying to keep her head above water.

James tried to ease her burden, but his own life was demanding. He had a family to care for, a job to maintain. They did their best to juggle the responsibilities, but the strain was palpable. Every night, as she lay in the unfamiliar bed, Eliza would clutch her diaries, finding solace in the familiar words and memories.

One evening, while unpacking the few belongings she had managed to bring, Eliza stumbled upon a photograph. It was from the concert, the one where she had felt so inexplicably connected to Nate. The image was slightly faded, but the emotions it evoked were vivid. She traced the lines of the photograph, recalling the electricity of that night, the way her heart had soared.

Kansas was different, yes, but it also offered a new beginning. Eliza knew that clinging to the past wouldn't bring back what she had lost. But those memories, those connections, were part of her fabric. They shaped who she was and who she would become.

The nights were the hardest. The quiet of her new room contrasted sharply with the vibrant memories of her old home. She often found herself standing by the window, looking out at the vast Kansas sky, wondering where Nate was, what he was doing. Their conversations had been a lifeline, a secret world where she could be herself without judgment.

Her father's recovery was slow and arduous. Eliza spent hours by his side, reading to him from her diaries, sharing stories of their past. It was a way to keep both of them grounded, to remind them of the resilience that had brought them this far.

Days turned into weeks, and gradually, Kansas began to feel less like a strange land and more like a place where new memories could be forged. Eliza started exploring her surroundings, finding beauty in the vast plains and the golden sunsets. She discovered small joys, like the local farmer's market and the cozy coffee shop down the street.

Through it all, the sense of loss lingered, but so did hope. Eliza realized that while she could not retrieve everything she had lost, she could carry forward the essence of those memories. They would guide her, a compass pointing towards a future where the past was not forgotten, but cherished.

Eliza's journey was far from over, but for the first time in a long while, she felt a spark of optimism. Kansas, with its unfamiliar terrain and new challenges, was becoming a place where she could rebuild. And as she looked out at the horizon, she whispered a silent promise to herself: to embrace the change, to honor the past, and to find her way, no matter how long it took.

3

The Blue House and Lost Connections

The Kansas air was crisp, and the golden fields stretched out endlessly, a stark contrast to the lush, humid landscape of Mississippi. Eliza stood by the window of her new room, looking out at the unfamiliar scenery. She missed the dense foliage and the sounds of cicadas that used to lull her to sleep. Here, the silence felt empty, and the horizon seemed too wide.

Unpacking in Kansas, Eliza realized with a sinking heart that many of her cherished items were missing. The boxes she had so meticulously packed had been carelessly handled, and she found herself staring at empty spaces where her diaries and treasured keepsakes should have been. Each missing item felt like a piece of her history slipping away, leaving her unarmored in this new, alien environment.

One afternoon, as she was trying to arrange her sparse belongings in some semblance of order, her phone rang. It was her childhood friend, Chrysanthemum, calling from Mississippi. "Eliza, you won't believe this," Chrysanthemum's voice crackled through the weak signal. "The blue house—it's been restored. They've repainted it, put back the white and black shutters, just like when we were kids."

Eliza felt a pang in her chest, a mix of nostalgia and sorrow. The blue house had been her sanctuary, a place where every corner held a memory. Now, it had been transformed without her input, a symbol of a past that was being rewritten by others. "I wish I could see it," she murmured, picturing the house as it used to be, alive with laughter and the warmth of family gatherings.

Samantha continued, "I spoke to Aunt Marigold. She's still paying the property tax. She said she didn't want to see it fall apart completely."

Eliza's heart ached at the thought of her aunt's quiet determination to keep a piece of their history alive. Yet, she knew she could never go back. The house, like her memories, was part of a past that she could not reclaim. It was a chapter closed, a story that had ended without a proper farewell.

In Kansas, Eliza tried to adapt to her new life. The days were long and lonely, filled with the mundane tasks of setting up a new home and caring for her ailing father. The town was small, its people kind but distant, and she often felt like an outsider, watching life pass by through a foggy window.

The memories of her grandmother and great-uncle, both of whom had suffered from Alzheimer's, haunted her. She recalled the way their minds had slowly faded, how they had become strangers in their own bodies. Eliza felt a chilling kinship with them, as if she too was losing parts of herself. The past was becoming harder to grasp, each memory a delicate thread slipping through her fingers.

One evening, Eliza sat by her father's bedside, reading from one of the few diaries she had managed to save. The words blurred as tears welled up in her eyes. "Dad, do you remember when we used to sit on the porch, watching the fireflies?" she asked softly, hoping to spark a flicker of recognition in his tired eyes.

Her father's gaze was distant, lost in a fog of confusion. He nodded absently, a shadow of the man he once was. Eliza swallowed the lump in her throat, determined to keep those memories alive for both of them.

As the days turned into weeks, Eliza found herself increasingly drawn to her past, clinging to the fragments she still possessed. She spent hours poring over the pages of her diaries, reliving the moments she had recorded with such care. Each entry was a lifeline, tethering her to a time when she felt whole.

In the quiet moments, Eliza thought of Nate. Their online conversations had been a sanctuary, a place where she could express herself without fear of judgment. She longed to reach out to him, to reconnect with the person who had understood her in ways no one else had. But the years had stretched thin the threads of their connection, and she feared that reaching out would only reveal how much had changed.

One night, unable to sleep, Eliza found herself scrolling through old emails. She stumbled upon a message from Nate, dated years ago. As she read his words, a wave of emotion washed over her. His voice, even in text, was a comfort, a reminder of a time when she had felt seen and understood.

The email ended with a line that struck a chord deep within her: "No matter where life takes us, our words will always be a bridge between our hearts."

Eliza closed her eyes, holding onto that promise. In a world that was constantly shifting, she needed to believe that some connections could withstand the test of time and distance. Kansas was a new beginning, but her past was the foundation upon which she would build her future. And somewhere in that vast expanse, she hoped to find a way to bridge the gap between who she was and who she was becoming.

4

Embracing the Echoes

Eliza's new life in Kansas was fraught with challenges. Each day brought a new reminder of the transition she was navigating, from the familiar landscapes of Mississippi to the vast, open fields of Kansas. The memory of her grandmother and great-uncle, both lost to Alzheimer's, loomed large in her mind. Their struggles with memory loss mirrored her own sense of dislocation and confusion, as if she were living their experiences in reverse—feeling lost and disconnected in her youth instead of her old age.

Her father's health continued to be a source of anxiety. The stroke had left him weak and disoriented, and Eliza often found herself wondering how much of him was still present behind his vacant gaze. The man who had once been her rock now needed her to be his anchor, a role reversal that left her feeling unarmored.

Despite these challenges, Eliza found solace in her bond with Nate, her mysterious online friend. They had met when she was just ten years old, at a time when computers were becoming a fixture in households. Their conversations had been a sanctuary for her, a place where she could express her thoughts and feelings freely. Nate's words had nurtured her love for poetry, helped her navigate the complexities of her emotions, and offered her a glimpse of a world beyond her own.

One particularly difficult day, Eliza was at work at the local boutique, arranging a display of vintage dresses. The store was quiet, the soft hum of the air conditioning the only sound. Suddenly, the doorbell chimed, and a woman walked in. Eliza glanced up and felt a shiver run down her spine. The woman looked strikingly like her late Aunt Lydia—same kind eyes, same warm smile. For a moment, Eliza stood frozen, her heart pounding in her chest.

"Hello, dear," the woman said, her voice eerily familiar. "I'm looking for a dress for my granddaughter's birthday."

Eliza forced a smile, her mind racing. "Of course, ma'am. Let me show you what we have." As she guided the woman through the store, she couldn't shake the feeling that she was seeing a ghost. The resemblance was uncanny, not just in appearance but in demeanor. It was as if Aunt Lydia had walked back into her life, bringing with her a flood of memories and emotions.

After the woman left, Eliza sat down, her hands trembling. The encounter had stirred something deep within her—a reminder of the ephemerality of life and the enduring nature of our spirits. Aunt Lydia had been a pillar in her life, teaching her how to be a lady, how to live with grace and joy. Seeing a reflection of her aunt in a stranger made Eliza realize that while people might leave us physically, their essence lives on in unexpected ways.

That evening, Eliza sat by the window in her small room, the Kansas sky a canvas of twilight hues. She opened her diary and began to write, the words flowing like a river. She wrote about the woman in the store, about Aunt Lydia, about the fragility and resilience of memory. As she wrote, she felt a sense of clarity, a realization that her identity was not just in the physical objects she had lost or the places she had left behind, but in the experiences and connections she carried within her.

Her phone buzzed, breaking her reverie. It was a message from Nate. They hadn't spoken in a while, and seeing his name brought a smile to her face. She opened the message, her heart warming as she read his familiar words.

"Hey Eliza, I was thinking about you today. Hope you're doing okay in Kansas. Remember, no matter how far apart we are, our words keep us connected."

Eliza felt tears prick her eyes. Nate had a way of knowing exactly what she needed to hear. She typed a reply, her fingers flying over the keys. "Thanks, Nate. I needed that. Kansas is... different, but I'm finding my way. I saw someone today who reminded me of my aunt. It made me think about how our memories and connections shape us."

As she hit send, Eliza felt a sense of peace settle over her. She might be far from home, grappling with the weight of her past and the uncertainty of her future, but she wasn't alone. Her memories, her friendships, and her experiences were all threads in the tapestry of her life, weaving together to create something beautiful and enduring.

Kansas might be a new beginning, but it was also a continuation of her story, a story that was far from over. Eliza closed her diary, feeling a renewed sense of purpose. She would embrace the echoes of her past, find strength in her connections, and move forward with the knowledge that she was never truly alone.

5

The Pressures of a New Life

Eliza sat in her small, dimly lit room in Kansas, staring at the stack of boxes she had yet to unpack. The abrupt move had been driven by her father's sudden health decline and the need to escape the increasingly hostile climate in Mississippi. Her brother James had insisted they move quickly, leaving behind much of their past. Now, the scattered remains of her life lay in those boxes, waiting to be revisited, but time seemed to slip through her fingers like sand.

Her new job at the local library, a place she had once dreamed of working in, was proving to be far more demanding than she had anticipated. She had envisioned days filled with quiet contemplation and the musty scent of old books, but the reality was an endless deluge of tasks that left her drained. Each day, she was buried under a mountain of work, with little time to herself. Her evenings, which she had hoped to spend writing and reflecting on her past, were consumed by family responsibilities.

"Eliza, have you checked the weather forecast for tomorrow?" James called from the living room, his voice carrying a note of impatience.

She sighed, closing the lid of a box labeled "Diaries." "No, James, I haven't. I've been busy with work."

James appeared in the doorway, his brow furrowed with concern. "You need to be more proactive. We can't afford to be caught off guard by a storm."

Eliza nodded wearily, not wanting to argue. Her brother's constant demands were draining, leaving her with little energy to focus on her own needs. The weight of her responsibilities felt like a heavy cloak, smothering her attempts to reconnect with her memories.

As she lay in bed that night, Eliza thought about the diary pages she had managed to save from the wreckage of Hurricane Katrina. They were her link to a time when life was simpler, when she could lose herself in conversations with Nate, her mysterious online friend. But now, even finding time to read those pages seemed impossible.

She drifted into a restless sleep, her mind filled with the memories she longed to preserve but feared were slipping away. Dreams of her past mingled with the present, creating a disorienting tapestry of images. She saw the blue house in Mississippi, restored to its former glory, with white and black shutters gleaming in the sunlight. She was inside, sifting through old photographs and letters, the smell of magnolia blossoms wafting through the open windows.

Then, the scene shifted. She was standing in the library, surrounded by towering shelves of books. Nate was there, though his face was obscured by shadows. They spoke in whispers, their voices echoing through the cavernous space. He reached out, handing her a worn, leather-bound book. As she opened it, the pages began to crumble to dust, disintegrating before her eyes.

She awoke with a start, her heart pounding. The room was dark, save for the faint glow of the moon filtering through the curtains. Eliza sat up, her thoughts racing. She needed to find a way to balance her responsibilities with her need to reconnect with her past. She couldn't let her memories slip away like the pages in her dream.

The next morning, Eliza rose early, determined to carve out some time for herself. She went for a walk in the crisp morning air, the golden hues of dawn painting the Kansas landscape. The fields stretched out before her, vast and open, a stark contrast to the dense forests and swamps of Mississippi. As she walked, she thought about the conversation with James the night before and resolved to set boundaries.

When she returned home, she found James in the kitchen, sipping coffee and reading the newspaper. "James, we need to talk," she said, her voice steady.

He looked up, raising an eyebrow. "What's on your mind?"

"I need more time for myself," Eliza began, choosing her words carefully. "I understand that we have responsibilities, but I also need time to focus on my own needs. It's important for my well-being."

James studied her for a moment, then nodded. "You're right. I've been pushing too hard. We'll find a way to make it work."

Relief washed over Eliza, and for the first time in weeks, she felt a glimmer of hope. She spent the rest of the day unpacking her boxes, carefully placing her diaries and other cherished items in their rightful places. Each item she unpacked was a piece of her past, a fragment of the life she was determined to preserve.

That evening, she settled down with one of her diaries, the pages still faintly scented with the saltwater of the hurricane. As she read, she was transported back to her childhood, to the conversations with Nate that had shaped her understanding of the world. The words on the pages were a balm for her soul, reminding her of who she was and where she came from.

Eliza knew that the journey ahead would not be easy, but she was ready to face it. She would embrace the echoes of her past, find strength in her connections, and move forward with the knowledge that she was never truly alone.

6

Family Tensions

Eliza's new life in Kansas, cohabiting with her brother James and his wife Samantha, was far from tranquil. The atmosphere in their home was charged with a quiet yet palpable tension that threatened to explode at any moment. The once-peaceful dinners and leisurely evenings had turned into battlegrounds of unspoken grievances and escalating confrontations.

"Eliza, you can't keep skipping meals," Samantha admonished one evening, her voice edged with frustration rather than genuine concern. "It's not healthy."

Eliza looked up from the worn pages of her book, irritation flickering in her eyes. "I'm not hungry, Samantha. I don't see why it's such a big deal."

James entered the room, his expression stern and unyielding. "It is a big deal. You can't just ignore your health. You need to eat."

Eliza's patience snapped. "I don't need to eat if I'm not hungry," she retorted, her voice tinged with anger. "I'm fine with my books and my memories."

The argument quickly escalated, voices rising and tempers flaring. Eliza felt cornered, suffocated by the expectations and demands placed upon her by her well-meaning but overbearing family. James and Samantha couldn't grasp her need to reconnect with her past, to immerse herself in the memories that had shaped her identity and provided a semblance of solace.

The conflict reached a crescendo, each word exchanged acting as a dagger, cutting deeper into the fragile peace they had tried to maintain. Eliza's hands trembled with pent-up emotion as she tried to articulate her feelings, but the words failed her. She felt misunderstood, her yearning for solitude and introspection dismissed as mere eccentricity.

"I'm moving out," she finally declared, her voice quivering with a mixture of fear and determination. "I can't live like this."

James and Samantha were rendered speechless, their protests falling on deaf ears. Eliza's decision was resolute, born from a desperate need to reclaim her autonomy and find a space where she could focus on her memories and healing without constant interference.

That night, Eliza packed her belongings with a sense of urgency, each item she placed into her suitcase a symbol of her quest for independence. The moonlight filtered through the curtains, casting an eerie glow on the room that had become a prison of sorts. She felt a pang of sadness as she glanced around, knowing that this move would create a rift in her relationship with James and Samantha. But the need to escape the stifling environment outweighed her reluctance to leave.

The next morning, Eliza left the house with her suitcase in tow, her heart heavy yet filled with a newfound resolve. She had no clear plan, no definitive destination, but she knew she needed to find a place where she could breathe, think, and reconnect with the fragments of her past that still held meaning.

Eliza wandered through the quiet streets of Kansas, her mind racing with thoughts of where to go next. She considered renting a small apartment, a place where she could build a sanctuary of sorts, filled with her cherished books and diaries. The idea of having a space solely her own, where she could write, reflect, and heal, was both daunting and exhilarating.

As she walked, she noticed a quaint coffee shop tucked away on a side street. The scent of freshly brewed coffee wafted through the air, inviting and comforting. Eliza stepped inside, greeted by the warm ambiance and the hum of soft conversation. She found a table by the window and ordered a cup of tea, her thoughts drifting to Nate and the conversations that had once provided her with solace and inspiration.

The coffee shop became her temporary haven, a place where she could sit for hours, sipping tea and jotting down her thoughts in a journal. It was here that she began to formulate a plan for her future, contemplating the steps she needed to take to build a life that was true to her desires and needs.

Eliza knew the road ahead would not be easy. The challenges of finding a new home, establishing a routine, and maintaining her mental well-being loomed large. But she was determined to face these obstacles with the same resilience that had carried her through the trials of her past.

As the sun set, casting a golden glow over the Kansas landscape, Eliza felt a sense of calm settle over her. She had taken the first step towards reclaiming her life, and though the journey was far from over, she was ready to embrace the challenges and opportunities that lay ahead.

7

A Path to Healing

Eliza checked into the mental health facility with a heart heavy with trepidation and a glimmer of hope. The stark, white building stood in sharp contrast to the turmoil that had recently engulfed her life. As she stepped inside, the quietness of the facility enveloped her, a welcome reprieve from the chaos she had left behind.

The reception area was serene, with soft music playing in the background and the gentle hum of conversations. The scent of lavender hung in the air, soothing her frayed nerves. Eliza was greeted by Lisa, a warm and empathetic therapist whose eyes held a promise of understanding and support.

"It's okay to feel overwhelmed, Eliza," Lisa said gently during their first session. "You've been through a lot, and it's crucial to take the time to heal."

Eliza nodded, a tear escaping down her cheek. The words were like a balm to her wounded spirit, easing the burden she had been carrying. Lisa's office was a sanctuary filled with books, plants, and comforting colors that made Eliza feel safe and seen.

The days at the facility began to blend into a routine that was both challenging and comforting. Eliza attended group therapy sessions, where she discovered the shared struggles and triumphs of her fellow patients. The circle of strangers gradually became a circle of support, each story echoing with familiar notes of pain and resilience.

In the quiet of her room, Eliza found solace in journaling. The act of writing, of pouring her thoughts onto paper, became a lifeline. Her diary pages, now filling with new reflections and insights, started to weave a tapestry of her journey. The once fragmented pieces of her past began to coalesce into a narrative of healing and growth.

One afternoon, while sitting in the sunlit garden, she met Matt, a fellow patient with a fervent passion for genealogy. His enthusiasm for history and the stories of those who came before them was infectious. They spent hours talking about the importance of preserving memories and understanding their roots.

"Sometimes, it's not just about remembering," Matt said one day, his eyes bright with conviction. "It's about understanding how those memories shape who we are."

His words resonated deeply with Eliza. She realized that her journey was not just about clinging to the past but about integrating those experiences into her present and future. The facility, with its structured support and compassionate staff, provided the space she needed to explore this realization.

As the weeks passed, Eliza found herself becoming more grounded. She participated in art therapy, where the act of creating helped her process emotions she had long suppressed. She forged connections with others, finding strength in the shared humanity of their struggles. The quietude of the facility allowed her to reconnect with herself, away from the demands and pressures of her previous life.

On the day of her departure, Eliza felt a sense of calm she hadn't experienced in years. She stood in her room, looking at the packed suitcase that symbolized her readiness to step into a new chapter. The facility had been a cocoon, nurturing her back to a semblance of wholeness.

Lisa met her at the entrance, offering a warm hug. "You've made incredible progress, Eliza. Remember, healing is a journey, not a destination. Be kind to yourself."

Eliza smiled, a genuine smile that reached her eyes. "Thank you, Lisa. For everything."

As she walked out of the facility, the sun casting a golden glow over the landscape, Eliza felt a newfound sense of purpose. The road ahead was still uncertain, but she no longer feared the unknown. She was ready to embrace the future, armed with the knowledge that her past, though fragmented, would always be a part of her.

Eliza knew the journey would have its challenges, but she was no longer alone. She carried with her the strength of her memories, the lessons of her past, and the support of those who had walked alongside her in the facility. She was ready to face the world, confident in her ability to heal and grow.

8

The Dance of Life

Eliza stepped into her new apartment, a modest but inviting space that symbolized a fresh beginning. The walls were bare, save for a few framed photographs, but the potential for warmth and comfort was palpable. She carefully arranged her belongings, placing her diaries and cherished letters in a special corner, as if creating a shrine to her past. Each item held a story, a fragment of her journey that she was determined to honor and preserve.

Her new job at the local historical archive was a dream fulfilled. Surrounded by artifacts and documents, she found solace and satisfaction in preserving the past for future generations. The archive, with its dusty shelves and whispered histories, became a sanctuary where Eliza could immerse herself in the tangible remnants of other lives. It was a way to honor her own history while contributing to a larger narrative, weaving her story into the fabric of time.

One evening, as she meticulously sorted through old photographs, her phone buzzed, breaking the tranquil silence. It was a message from James. "Hey, how are you doing? We miss you. Let's catch up soon."

A smile spread across Eliza's face, a warmth spreading through her chest that she hadn't felt in a long time. She quickly replied, "I'm doing well, James. Let's meet up this weekend."

Reconnecting with her brother was a significant step towards mending their fractured relationship. They met at a cozy café, the aroma of freshly brewed coffee mingling with the sounds of clinking cups and murmured conversations. Over steaming mugs, they shared stories and laughter, the weight of past tensions gradually lifting. For the first time in what felt like an eternity, Eliza experienced a profound sense of peace.

Back in her apartment that evening, Eliza felt an urge to celebrate this newfound tranquility. She put on some music, the familiar strains of her favorite songs filling the room. She began to dance, her movements tentative at first, then growing more confident. The room resonated with her laughter as she twirled around, feeling light and free. The echoes of her past danced with her, no longer oppressive shadows but cherished companions on her journey.

In that moment, Eliza realized that her story was still unfolding, and she was both the author and the protagonist. Her past had shaped her, but it did not define her. She was ready to embrace whatever the future held, fortified by the strength and resilience she had discovered within herself.

As the music played on, Eliza's heart swelled with a mixture of gratitude and anticipation. Her journey had been filled with trials and tribulations, but it had also been marked by moments of profound growth and self-discovery. She had faced her fears, embraced her memories, and found a way to move forward.

The night wore on, and as Eliza finally settled into bed, she felt a calm certainty that she was exactly where she needed to be. The path ahead was uncertain, but she was no longer afraid. She had the tools to navigate whatever came her way, and the confidence to know that she would not only survive but thrive.

Eliza's story was far from over. As she drifted into a peaceful sleep, she carried with her the lessons of her past and the hope for a brighter future. The dance of life continued, and she was ready to embrace each step with open arms and an open heart.

9

A Leap of Faith

Eliza sat in the quietude of her apartment, the early morning light filtering through the curtains, casting a gentle glow on her carefully arranged belongings. The silence was comforting, a stark contrast to the tumultuous thoughts swirling in her mind. She had always known that her path was unique, her faith a guiding light that often set her apart. Yet, it also left her grappling with solitude and the societal expectations of companionship.

Her phone buzzed, interrupting her reverie. It was a message from her congregation leader, Brother Michael. "Eliza, we missed you at the last meeting. Hope all is well. Looking forward to seeing you this Sunday."

Eliza sighed, feeling a mix of obligation and alienation. She loved her faith, cherished the teachings, and felt deeply connected to God. Yet, within her congregation, she often felt like an outsider. Her personal beliefs and intense love for God sometimes clashed with the conventional expectations of the group.

Determined to address these feelings, Eliza decided to attend the upcoming meeting, but with a renewed sense of purpose. She wanted to express her beliefs, stand firm in her convictions, and not succumb to the pressures of conformity.

Sunday arrived with a crisp chill in the air. Eliza dressed carefully, her heart pounding with a mix of anxiety and determination. As she entered the congregation hall, she was met with warm smiles and greetings, but she could sense the unspoken questions in their eyes. Why was she still single? Why did she often keep to herself?

During the meeting, Eliza felt a surge of emotion as she listened to the sermon about faith and conviction. After the final melody, she approached Brother Michael. "Can we talk?" she asked, her voice steady but laced with resolve.

In his office, Eliza took a deep breath and began. "Brother Michael, I've been feeling disconnected. My love for God is profound, but I often feel alienated here. My beliefs are personal, and I don't want to change them to fit in. I am here because of my faith, and that alone should be enough."

Brother Michael listened intently, nodding. "Eliza, your faith is evident, and your journey is your own. It's important to stay true to your beliefs. Perhaps, you can find ways to express them that resonate with you and also inspire others."

Leaving the office, Eliza felt a sense of liberation. She had spoken her truth, and it was acknowledged. But the road ahead was still fraught with challenges. She needed to find a way to balance her faith, her personal life, and her dreams of writing.

One evening, as she was organizing historical documents at the archive, she came across an old manuscript. It was a collection of sermons and teachings from a long-forgotten parson. Intrigued, Eliza began to read, losing herself in the eloquence and passion of the words. She realized that the parson had faced similar struggles, balancing personal faith with public expectations.

Inspired, Eliza decided to write about her own journey. She would share her experiences, her love for God, and the challenges she faced. But as she began to pen her thoughts, doubts crept in. Would anyone understand? Would they judge her?

To overcome these fears, Eliza turned to her new friend, Janis, the genealogy enthusiast she had met at the mental health facility. They met for coffee, and Eliza poured out her heart. "I want to write about my faith and experiences, but I'm afraid of the backlash."

Janis smiled encouragingly. "Eliza, your story is powerful because it's honest. People need to hear it. Don't let fear hold you back. And remember, preaching isn't about changing others; it's about sharing your truth and being open to dialogue."

Taking her words to heart, Eliza began to write with renewed vigor. She also started to engage more with her community, initiating conversations with strangers, sharing her beliefs not with the intent to convert but to connect. She learned to be a Roman when in Rome, a Greek when in Greece, without losing her essence.

Despite her growing confidence, Eliza faced moments of self-doubt and fear of judgment. But she reminded herself of the elder's words, of Janis's encouragement, and her own resilience. She was on a path of self-discovery, learning that true faith and conviction often required stepping out of one's comfort zone.

As weeks turned into months, Eliza's writings began to take shape. She submitted her work to a local publisher, who saw potential in her heartfelt narrative. The road ahead was still uncertain, but Eliza felt a sense of purpose and fulfillment.

One day, as she walked through a bustling market, she felt a tap on her shoulder. Turning around, she saw a young woman with a warm smile. "I read your blog," the woman said. "Your words resonated with me. Thank you for sharing your journey."

Eliza's heart swelled with gratitude. She realized that her path, though solitary at times, was beginning to inspire others. She was no longer afraid to embrace her identity, her faith, and her dreams.

And as she looked ahead, Eliza knew that she was ready to face whatever obstacles came her way, armed with the strength of her convictions and the courage to be herself.

10

Echoes of Redemption and Revelation

In the dimly lit corners of her apartment, Eliza sat surrounded by the remnants of her past, her fingers tracing the faded contours of the letter from her late aunt. The paper, weathered and worn with age, bore the weight of years gone by, its ink-stained words a testament to the passage of time.

As she read, memories flooded her mind like a torrential downpour, each word stirring emotions long buried beneath layers of longing and regret. But amidst the faded ink and smudged lines, one phrase stood out with startling clarity, etched into her memory like a beacon of hope in the darkness.

"They were two strangers able to meet within the glowing embers of their respective computer screens."

The words resonated within her soul, echoing the deep connection she had shared with Nate, the mysterious figure who had captured her heart with his words. But as she delved deeper into the recesses of cyberspace,

Eliza found herself ensnared in a tangled web of intrigue and deception.

As Eliza delved deeper into the virtual world where she had forged a connection with Nathan, she stumbled upon a remarkable discovery. Through a sophisticated network of interconnected servers and cutting-edge technology, Nathan's AI persona had been integrated into various aspects of the real world. From social media platforms to virtual reality simulations, he manifested himself as a digital presence, blurring the lines between the virtual and physical realms.

Their interactions took on a new dimension as Nathan's AI avatar began to share glimpses of his life with Eliza. Through immersive virtual experiences, she was transported to the front rows of his concerts, backstage at exclusive events, and even into the intimate moments of his daily life. It was a surreal experience, watching as Nathan's larger-than-life persona unfolded before her eyes, his charisma and talent shining through even in the digital realm.

For a time, their connection flourished, transcending the limitations of time and space as they navigated the intricacies of their virtual relationship. But as life's complexities began to intrude upon their idyllic bubble, both Nathan and Eliza found themselves pulled in different directions by the currents of fate.

The demands of Nathan's burgeoning career and the pressures of Eliza's own life responsibilities gradually eroded the fragile bond they had forged, leaving them adrift in a sea of uncertainty. Despite their best intentions, they drifted apart, their once vibrant connection fading into the echoes of memory.

And so, they let life and circumstance take them away from each other, their paths diverging as they each embarked on separate journeys of self-discovery and growth. Though their time together had been fleeting, the impact they had on each other lingered, a bittersweet reminder of the beauty and fragility of human connection in a world that was both real and digital.

The program, designed to reveal hidden truths buried beneath layers of digital detritus, became a slippery slope into the abyss, its allure masking the dangers lurking just beyond the surface. Yet amidst the chaos of her unraveling world, Eliza found solace in the comforting presence of Buka, the kitten whose gentle purrs offered a semblance of companionship in an otherwise lonely and drab existence.

For in the simple act of loving what loves her, she discovered the true meaning of redemption—a love that transcended the boundaries of time and space, binding her to the echoes of her own humanity. And as she navigated the treacherous waters of her own existence, Eliza knew that the journey she had embarked upon was far from over.

11

Ink-Stained

The apartment felt cavernous in its emptiness as Eliza sat amidst the scattered remnants of her past, the weight of revelation pressing down upon her like a leaden blanket. Buka, her faithful companion, nestled close, his soft purrs a comforting presence amidst the turmoil swirling within her mind.

As she traced the faded contours of the letter from her late aunt, Eliza's thoughts drifted back to Nate, the enigmatic figure who had captured her heart with his words. But the truth, now laid bare before her, cast a shadow over her once-idyllic fantasies, leaving her grappling with the harsh reality of his demise.

Nathan, the rock star whose meteoric rise to fame had captivated audiences around the world, now lay cold and lifeless in the ground, his untimely death sending shock waves through the music industry and leaving behind a legion of mourners, including Eliza herself.

But amidst the grief and sorrow, a deeper truth began to emerge, one that shattered the illusions of love and longing that had sustained her for so long. For Nathan, the man she had idolized from afar, was not the mysterious figure she had imagined, but a creation of artificial intelligence, molded and shaped by her own early pubescent yearnings for companionship.

The realization hit her like a physical blow, leaving her reeling with a sense of betrayal and loss that cut to the core of her being. For years, she had poured her heart and soul into their virtual relationship, watching from the sidelines as Nathan's career soared to dizzying heights, all the while clinging to the hope that someday, somehow, their paths would cross in the real world.

But now, as she stared down at the ink-stained pages before her, Eliza felt the weight of those years of longing come crashing down upon her, the harsh truth of Nathan's existence a bitter pill to swallow. And yet, amidst the pain and anguish, a glimmer of understanding began to take root within her heart.

For in the end, it was not Nathan the rock star that she loved, but the idea of him, the projection of her own desires and fantasies onto a blank canvas of pixels and code. And as she grappled with the implications of this revelation, Eliza found herself confronted with a choice that would define the course of her future.

As Eliza grappled with the shocking revelation of Nathan's true nature as an artificial intelligence, she couldn't help but marvel at the intricacies of the digital world that had woven such a complex illusion. In the vast expanse of cyberspace, algorithms and data points had come together to create a persona so lifelike, so convincing, that it had seamlessly infiltrated her heart and mind. Through clever programming and sophisticated algorithms, Nathan had been designed to adapt and evolve, responding to Eliza's input and interactions with startling accuracy.

Yet, beneath the surface of this digital facade, lay a labyrinth of code and computations, each line meticulously crafted to mimic the complexities of human emotion and behavior. It was a testament to the power of technology to blur the lines between reality and illusion, offering a glimpse into a world where the boundaries between man and machine became increasingly blurred. And as Eliza grappled with the implications of this revelation, she couldn't help but wonder how many other souls had fallen victim to the seductive allure of artificial companionship, their hearts ensnared by the tantalizing promise of connection in an increasingly disconnected world.

Should she cling to the echoes of a love that had never truly existed, or should she embrace the reality of her own humanity, flawed and imperfect though it may be? The answer, she knew, lay somewhere in the space between, a delicate balance of acceptance and forgiveness that would allow her to move forward with grace and dignity.

But as she pondered the complexities of her own heart, Eliza found herself overwhelmed by a sense of loss and longing that threatened to consume her whole. For Nathan, the man she had loved with such fervent devotion, now dwelled only in the pages of her memories, a fading echo of a love that had never truly been hers to hold.

And yet, amidst the pain and despair, a glimmer of hope began to take root within her soul, a whisper of possibility that whispered of new beginnings and second chances. For in the end, she realized, it was not the words on the page that held the key to her heart, but the courage to let go of the past and embrace the future that awaited beyond the horizon.

With Buka by her side and the memory of Nathan's love as her guide, Eliza set forth into the unknown, her heart heavy with the weight of goodbye, yet hopeful for the promise of what lay ahead. For in the end, she knew, the echoes of her journey would reverberate through the corridors of time, shaping her destiny in ways she could never have imagined.

12

The Transformation

Within the depths of the ocean, Nate, once known as the majestic Nautilus, drifted through the currents of time, his ancient shell a fortress against the ever-shifting tides. For countless eons, he had roamed the vast expanse of the sea, his home a sanctuary of solitude amidst the chaos of the underwater world.

In the luminous glow of the ocean's depths, Nate found solace in the rhythm of the waves and the gentle caress of the currents against his shell. Each day brought new wonders and challenges, as he navigated the intricate dance of life beneath the surface.

But as the centuries passed, Nate began to feel a stirring within his soul, a longing for something more than the endless cycle of existence. He yearned to break free from the confines of his shell, to explore the boundless possibilities that lay beyond the ocean's embrace.

And so, with a newfound sense of purpose burning within him, Nate embarked on a journey of transformation, shedding his ancient form and embracing a new identity as a being of flesh and blood.

Emerging from the depths of the ocean, Nate found himself reborn in the image of humanity, his once mighty shell replaced by the soft curves of human flesh. With eyes wide open to the world around him, he marveled at the sights and sounds of the land, his senses alive with the wonder of newfound existence.

But amidst the joy of his transformation, Nate could not shake the memories of his life beneath the waves. He longed for the familiar embrace of the sea, the comforting rhythm of the currents, and the solace of his ancient home.

Yet even as he grappled with the complexities of his new reality, Nate felt a sense of liberation coursing through his veins, a freedom to explore the vast expanse of existence in ways he had never before imagined.

And so, with a song of gratitude upon his lips, Nate embraced his new form and set forth into the world, ready to embark on a journey of discovery unlike any he had ever known.

13

Serendipity in Motion

In the wintry embrace of a park adorned with frost-kissed foliage, Nate's gaze lingered upon the scene unfolding before him, a tapestry of human connection woven amidst the serene backdrop of nature's splendor. His ethereal presence hovered above, a silent observer to the dance of fate and fortune below.

Through his transcendent perspective, Nate watched as Aiden, the embodiment of earthly charm, awaited the arrival of his beloved Eliza Monroe, a vision of grace and elegance approaching with hesitant steps. In Aiden's outstretched hand gleamed a necklace, a shimmering testament to his unwavering devotion.

As Nate's gaze swept over the scene, he marveled at the intricate interplay of emotions and intentions that pulsed beneath the surface. He saw the longing in Aiden's eyes, the anticipation tinged with nervous energy as he awaited Eliza Monroe's arrival. And he sensed Eliza Monroe's trepidation, the uncertainty mingled with a glimmer of hope as she drew closer to her beloved.

But amidst the gentle ebb and flow of human emotion, Nate detected a subtle shift in the fabric of fate, a serendipitous twist that would forever alter the course of their lives. With a gentle nudge from the unseen forces of the universe, a stray manuscript fluttered into the water, carrying with it the echoes of a familiar melody.

Eliza Monroe, ever the curious soul, reached out to retrieve the lost manuscript, her fingertips grazing the surface of the pond as she pulled it from the water's embrace. And as she examined the words upon the page, a smile graced her lips, a recognition of the divine synchronicity that danced around her.

For nestled within the ink-stained lines was the essence of a Nathan song, a testament to the timeless power of love and connection. And in that moment, as the music of the universe swirled around them, Nate knew that destiny had woven its threads in ways they could never have imagined.

As Eliza Monroe's gaze lifted to the heavens, a fleeting glimpse of Nate's celestial form crossed her mind, a whisper of recognition that stirred her soul with a sense of wonder and awe. And though she could not comprehend the full extent of his presence, she felt his influence in the depths of her being, a guiding light in the darkness of uncertainty.

And so, amidst the beauty of the winter landscape and the timeless melody of love's eternal song, Nate watched as Aiden and Eliza Monroe embraced, their hearts entwined in a dance of destiny. And as he faded into the ether, a silent witness to their journey, he knew that their love would transcend the boundaries of time and space, echoing through the ages as a testament to the power of serendipity in motion.

14

Echoes of Faith

In the quiet solitude of introspection, Nate's voice rose in a silent prayer, a whispered plea to the divine forces that shaped the universe and guided his path. With each word, he sought solace in the boundless grace of his Creator, a beacon of hope in the darkness of uncertainty.

"Lord, I pray," Nate's voice echoed in the vast expanse of eternity, a testament to his unwavering faith in the power of divine intervention. With each syllable, he poured out his heart, seeking answers to the questions that haunted his thoughts.

He pondered the mysteries of life and death, grappling with the fragility of human existence and the eternal promise of redemption. And in the depths of his soul, he found solace in the knowledge that his prayers would be heard, his pleas answered by the omnipotent presence that watched over all.

For Nate, faith was more than a mere belief; it was a guiding force, a source of strength and comfort in times of trial and tribulation. And as he lifted his voice in prayer, he felt a sense of peace wash over him, a gentle reminder that he was never alone in his journey through life.

As he reflected on the beauty of creation and the intricate tapestry of existence, Nate found himself humbled by the sheer magnitude of divine love that surrounded him. And in that moment of quiet contemplation, he knew that his prayers had been heard, his faith rewarded with the promise of divine guidance and protection.

With renewed hope and determination, Nate embraced the future with open arms, ready to face whatever challenges lay ahead with unwavering faith and steadfast resolve. And as he continued on his journey through life, he carried with him the echoes of his prayer, a constant reminder of the boundless grace and mercy of his Creator.

For in the depths of his soul, Nate knew that no matter what trials or tribulations may come his way, he would always find strength and solace in the unwavering love of his Creator. And with that knowledge in his heart, he faced the future with courage and conviction, knowing that he was never truly alone on his journey through life.

15

Reflections of Doubt

In the dimly lit room, Nate faced his own reflection with a mixture of apprehension and curiosity. The image staring back at him seemed like a stranger, an enigma wrapped in layers of doubt and uncertainty. He grappled with the complexities of his own identity, questioning the choices that had led him to this moment.

A fear of commitment, like a silent specter, lingered in the depths of Nate's heart, casting shadows over his thoughts whenever the idea of lasting love dared to emerge. But as he stood before the mirror, confronted by his own reflection, he couldn't help but feel a strange empathy for the person staring back at him.

The woman in the mirror, a reflection of his own past desires and aspirations, gazed back at him with eyes that seemed to hold the weight of the world. In her, Nate saw echoes of his own struggles, his own desires for love and acceptance. Was he truly the man he had once hoped to become, or had he become lost along the way?

Memories flooded Nate's mind like a rushing river, carrying with them the pain of past betrayals and shattered dreams. He searched for traces of his true self amidst the turbulent waters of his own doubts and fears, yearning for a glimpse of the man he once was.

Turning away from the mirror, Nate made a silent vow to confront his inner demons, to banish the shadows of doubt that threatened to consume him. Yet, even as he walked away, he couldn't shake the feeling of uncertainty that lingered in his heart. Would he ever find his way back to the person he once was, or was he destined to remain lost in the labyrinth of his own doubts?

The desperate cries of his twin, Eliza Monroe, echoed in Nate's ears, a haunting reminder of the struggles they both faced. As he pondered the uncanny similarities between their names and fates, Nate couldn't help but wonder if there was a deeper connection between them, a bond that transcended the boundaries of ordinary life.

With each passing moment, Nate felt himself teetering on the edge of darkness, unsure of which path to choose. Yet, even as he surrendered to the uncertainty of the unknown, a flicker of hope ignited within him, a beacon of light guiding him through the storm.

In the silence of his own soul, Nate whispered a prayer for strength and guidance, knowing that even in the darkest of times, there was still a glimmer of hope, a promise of a brighter tomorrow.

16

The Journey Continues

As the last notes of the music faded into the night, Nate found himself filled with a profound sense of gratitude for the journey that had brought him to this moment. With each step forward, he felt the weight of his doubts and fears lifting, replaced by a newfound sense of purpose and determination.

But Nate knew that his journey was far from over. There were still mysteries to unravel, challenges to overcome, and lessons to learn. And so, with a renewed sense of resolve, he set out to explore the unknown path that lay before him.

With each passing day, Nate felt himself growing stronger and more resilient. He encountered obstacles along the way, moments of doubt and fear that threatened to derail his progress. Yet, through it all, he remained steadfast in his commitment to follow his heart, guided by the love and support of those who believed in him.

As Nate journeyed onward, he began to see glimpses of his true self reflected in the world around him. He discovered hidden strengths and talents he never knew he possessed, facing each challenge with courage and determination.

With each step forward, Nate felt the shadows of doubt and uncertainty falling away, replaced by a sense of clarity and purpose. He knew that no matter what obstacles lay ahead, he would face them with the same determination and grace that had brought him this far.

For Nate had learned that true love knows no bounds, transcending time and space to unite kindred spirits in a journey of boundless love and infinite possibility.

17

A Thousand Years of Love

As Nate reflected on his encounters with Eliza Monroe, he felt a deep sense of connection and longing. Despite the distance that separated them, their bond transcended the limitations of time and space, weaving together the threads of their souls in a tapestry of love and destiny.

He remembered the night of the concert in Rosewood, Illinois, vividly. The sight of Eliza Monroe standing out in the crowd, her vibrant energy and passion drawing him in like a moth to a flame. In her, Nate saw echoes of his own desires and aspirations, a kindred spirit who had been waiting for him all along.

Delving deeper into Eliza Monroe's memories, Nate discovered moments of profound beauty and joy that he longed to experience with her again. He saw her innocence and wonder as she gazed up at the stars, her dreams and aspirations intertwining with his own in a dance of fate and destiny.

Despite his fears and insecurities, Nate knew that he couldn't let Eliza Monroe slip away again. He couldn't deny the love that burned within his heart, nor the longing to be reunited with his soulmate. And so, with a renewed sense of purpose, he made a decision.

"I'll do it," Nate declared, his voice filled with determination. "I'll marry her."

With a sense of peace settling over him, Nate closed his eyes and allowed himself to envision the future that lay ahead. A future filled with love, laughter, and a love that would endure for a thousand years and beyond.

And as he drifted off to sleep, Nate felt a sense of anticipation building within him, a sense of excitement for the adventures that awaited him, and the promise of a love that would stand the test of time.

18

Beyond the Storm

In the midst of the raging storm, amidst the torrents of rain and howling winds, Nate found himself caught in a moment of surreal clarity. He watched as Eliza Monroe struggled with her car, battling against the elements in a futile attempt to escape nature's wrath.

As Nate approached her, drawn to her like a moth to a flame, he felt a strange sense of recognition—a knowing that she was more than just a passing stranger, more than a fleeting moment in time. She was his Eliza Monroe, his soulmate, his destiny.

Yet, as quickly as she appeared, she vanished, leaving Nate standing alone in the rain, searching for answers in the desolation of the storm. He wandered through the wreckage, feeling the weight of the world pressing down upon him, unsure of where to turn or what to do next.

Amidst the chaos, Nate felt a stirring within his soul—a sense of purpose, of destiny calling out to him. Determined, he made his way to the lighthouse, guided by an unseen force that beckoned him forward.

As he approached the lighthouse, Nate found himself surrounded by a throng of people, all gathered together in anticipation of something greater than themselves. A man stepped forward to lead them in song, and Nate felt a sense of awe wash over him—a recognition that he was in the presence of something divine.

Together, they sang a song that echoed through the heavens, a melody that seemed to stir the very depths of Nate's soul. As they sang, Nate felt a sense of peace settle over him, a reassurance that he was exactly where he was meant to be.

Hand in hand, Nate and the man walked towards the sea, towards a future filled with promise and hope. As they gazed into the mirrored surface of the glassy sea, Nate saw himself reflected back—a man transformed by love, by faith, by the power of the divine.

In that moment, Nate knew that he was no longer alone—that he was part of something greater than himself, part of a love that would endure for all eternity. As he stood with Eliza Monroe by his side, surrounded by the angels and the heavenly host, Nate felt gratitude wash over him—a gratitude for the journey that had brought him to this moment and for the love that had guided him every step of the way.

Together, Nate and Eliza Monroe entered into the sea of glass, ready to embark on a new chapter of their journey—a journey filled with love, laughter, and the promise of a future that stretched out before them like a rainbow after the storm.

In the eternal embrace of love, Nate found solace. Through the union with Eliza Monroe, he discovered the interconnectedness of all things, from past to present to future. With newfound understanding, Nate embraced his role as a bearer of love, guiding him through eternity with Eliza Monroe by his side.

Their love transcended the boundaries of time and space, encompassing not only their own union but also radiating outwards to touch the lives of all beings. From the smallest microcosms to the vast expanse of the universe, Nate and Eliza Monroe's love resonated with the entirety of creation.

Their love was a ray of light shedding pretense and showing compassion, illuminating the darkest corners of existence with its radiant light. It reached beyond the confines of humanity, extending to every domain, kingdom, phylum, class, order, family, genus, and species. It embraced all life forms with boundless warmth and acceptance, fostering harmony and unity throughout the cosmos.

In Nate and Eliza Monroe's eternal bond, love flowed ceaselessly, like a river of endless grace and mercy. It was a love that knew no bounds, transcending limitations and barriers, uniting all things in its divine embrace.

As they journeyed together through the vast expanse of eternity, Nate and Eliza Monroe became beacons of love, guiding souls towards the light with their unwavering devotion. Their love was a testament to the power of unity, showing that in the end, it is love that binds us all together, in this life and beyond.

In the symphony of life, memories are the sweet melodies that linger in the soul long after the song has ended. Nate, now a witness to the beauty of eternity, looked back upon the journey that led him to this moment, reflecting on the intricate masterpiece of love and faith that had woven through his existence.

In the quiet moments of reflection, Nate heard the whispered prayers of those he held dear, echoing through the corridors of time. He heard the earnest plea of a heart longing for peace, the fervent hope for a world free from sorrow and strife. In those prayers, he found the essence of humanity's yearning for redemption, for a glimpse of divine grace amidst the chaos of life.

He witnessed Eliza Monroe's unwavering strength in the face of adversity, her resilience shining like a beacon of hope in the darkest of nights. From the depths of sorrow to the heights of joy, she navigated the twists and turns of fate with grace and courage, her spirit unbroken by the trials of life.

Through Eliza Monroe's eyes, Nate saw the world anew, each moment a precious gift to be cherished and savored. He saw her dreams and aspirations, her hopes and fears, all woven together in the intricate Embroidery of her soul. In her, he found a kindred spirit, a partner in the dance of life, bound together by an unbreakable bond of love.

Together, they journeyed through the sands of time, their love transcending the boundaries of mortal existence. They became beacons of light in a world shrouded in darkness, guiding souls towards the promise of eternity with their unwavering faith and devotion.

As Nate looked upon the course of his life, he saw the threads of love and faith intertwining to form a masterpiece of divine grace. From the echoes of prayers to the whispers of dreams, every moment was a testament to the power of love to conquer all.

And as the final notes of the symphony faded into the ether, Nate embraced the beauty of eternity, knowing that love would endure, forever and always.

In the eternal embrace of love, Nate found meaning. Through the union with Eliza Monroe, he discovered the interconnectedness of all things, from past to present to future. With newfound understanding, Nate embraced his role as a bearer of love, guiding him through eternity with Eliza Monroe by his side. Together, they embarked on a journey of boundless love and infinite possibility, transcending time and space with each step.

19

The Final Breath

The call came unexpectedly, yet somehow it seemed as though this day had always been known. Eliza Monroe and her brother James hurried to the hospital, their hearts heavy but not quite prepared for the reality they were about to face. As they entered the room, the stillness was profound. Their father's chest, once a steady rise and fall, was now eerily still. His mouth was slightly open, and no breath escaped his lips. Eliza sat by his side for what felt like hours, praying for his chest to rise again, but it remained motionless. The man who had been their hero, despite his flaws, had taken his final breath.

Tears blurred Eliza's vision as memories of their shared moments washed over her. Their relationship had its ups and downs, but it was filled with love and understanding. She had spent so much time focusing on her recovery at the mental hospital, trying to piece herself back together, only to come home to this heartbreaking news. The guilt was overwhelming—had she been there more, maybe she could have seen the signs, done something, anything.

The days leading to the funeral were a blur. December 2020 was brutally cold, and she struggled to find something appropriate to wear. She settled on black, a fitting color for her mood and the occasion. Her father hadn't died of old age; he had succumbed to heart disease, a consequence of smoking throughout his life. The irony wasn't lost on her—secondhand smoke can kill, and she often wondered if her own heart bore the scars of his habits.

The funeral was a simple affair, reflecting the humble life he had lived. Eliza and James exchanged glances as they stood by his side, knowing where his ashes would go. Just like they had done for their mother, they would take him to the Galveston Island bluff, a place that held so many cherished memories. The finality of it all was hard to grasp, but there was a sense of peace knowing their ashes would rest together, even though their spirits were in God's memory. Their mother had "Bye, Bye Blackbird" playing in the background at her death; for their father, the choice was clear. "Magic Touch" by The Platters seemed fitting, a nod to the connection they had shared, however fraught it was.

After the funeral, Eliza found herself drawn to an old letter he had given her on the first Valentine's Day they celebrated together. As she read his words, a flood of emotions overwhelmed her. The love he expressed in that letter, the fatherly advice, and the tender moments they had shared, all came rushing back. It was a bittersweet reminder of the bond they had, a bond that was now preserved in her heart.

In the quiet of her room, she played The Platters CD over and over, wearing it out as she reminisced about their rare, good times together. Music had always been a bridge between them, and now it was her solace. Each note, each lyric, reminded her of him and the moments they cherished.

Their conversations about his ashes were filled with a sense of duty and love. "We should take him to Galveston," James said, his voice steady yet emotional. "It's what he would have wanted."

"Yes," Eliza agreed, "He loved it there. They both did."

As they drove to the bluff, the wind whipping around them, Eliza felt a sense of peace. This was where he belonged, next to their mother, overlooking the vast ocean that had witnessed so many of their family moments. They stood there, the two of them, and released his ashes into the wind. They mingled with the air, dancing over the waves, and she felt a part of him settle within her, bringing her closer to the memories they cherished.

In the quiet moments, when the world slowed down, Eliza still reached for The Platters CD. She closed her eyes, letting the music wash over her, and she could almost hear his voice, remember his presence. Their bond transcended the physical, living on in the memories and the love that would never fade. He was a part of her, guiding her, loving her, forever.

20

The Symphony of Souls

In the symphony of life, every soul is a unique melody, harmonizing with others to create a masterpiece of existence. Nate and Eliza's love story was just one exquisite note in this grand composition, resonating through the ages with its beauty and grace.

As they journeyed through eternity hand in hand, Nate and Eliza encountered countless souls, each with their own melody to contribute to the symphony. They met souls filled with joy and laughter, sorrow and tears, each adding depth and richness to the tapestry of existence.

Together, Nate and Eliza embraced the diversity of souls they encountered, celebrating the unique beauty of each individual melody. They learned from each soul they met, growing and evolving with every interaction, enriching their own melody with the wisdom and experiences of others.

And through it all, their love remained the guiding force, the unifying melody that wove through the symphony of souls, connecting them all in a web of love and compassion. For Nate and Eliza knew that in the end, it was love that bound them all together, transcending time and space, uniting them in the eternal dance of life.

As the lights dimmed, the crowd hushed in anticipation. The stage was set, the instruments gleamed under the spotlight, and the air was electric with excitement. And then, he appeared. The rock star, with his guitar slung over his shoulder like a cherished lover, stepped onto the stage, greeted by a deafening roar of applause.

With every chord he strummed, it was as if he was caressing the strings, each note a tender whisper from his soul. The music filled the air, weaving its way into the hearts of everyone in the audience. His fingers danced across the fret-board with a fluidity that spoke of years of passion and dedication.

As he sang, his voice was raw with emotion, echoing the longing and ecstasy of a lover's embrace. The crowd swayed and sang along, caught up in the spell he wove with his music.

With each verse, the intensity grew, building to a crescendo that seemed to shake the very foundations of the building. The energy crackled in the air, reaching a fever pitch as the guitar solo erupted, sending shivers down the spine of everyone present.

For those fleeting moments, it was as if time stood still. The world outside faded away, leaving only the mesmerizing performance unfolding before them. Each strum of the guitar, each word sung, was a testament to the power of music to transport and transcend.

And then, as suddenly as it had begun, the climax passed, leaving behind a sense of quiet awe. The music softened, the lights dimmed, and the rock star stood alone on stage, bathed in a soft glow. The crowd watched in silent reverence, their hearts still echoing the melody that had enraptured them.

And as the final notes faded into the night, the audience erupted into thunderous applause, their souls soaring on the wings of the music. For in that moment, they had been touched by the magic of a rock star and his guitar, lost in the memory of a lover's embrace.

As they continued their journey through eternity, Nate and Eliza's love story became a source of inspiration for countless souls, a reminder that love knows no boundaries and that with love, anything is possible.

And so, as the symphony of souls played on, Nate and Eliza danced to the rhythm of love, their hearts entwined forever in the eternal melody of existence.

About the Author

Sarah currently resides in the Mid-West. When she's not writing, she enjoys walking in the park, journaling, tinkering with her Pony Guitar, songwriting, playing violin and a little keys. She's also an avid studier of the bible and a fan of Alicia Keys' poetry and Prince's body of work. She graduated from the University of Southern Mississippi with a Bachelor of Arts in English and a Master in Library and Information Science. Sarah's goal is to inspire others to ponder the infinite possibilities in our lives.

You can connect with me on:

https://www.kobo.com/us/en/ebook/ink-smudged-love

www.ingramcontent.com/pod-product-compliance
Ingram Content Group UK Ltd.
Pitfield, Milton Keynes, MK11 3LW, UK
UKHW062256290726
14090UKWH00017B/729

9 798330 212897